This Book Belongs To

_____

ATLANTIS

GOOD TIMES!

SIMON AND SCHUSTER/NICKELODEON

Stephen Hillenburg

Based on the TV series *SpongeBob SquarePants* created by Stephen Hillenburg
as seen on Nickelodeon

SIMON AND SCHUSTER
First published in Great Britain in 2010 by Simon & Schuster UK Ltd
1st Floor, 222 Gray's Inn Road, London WC1X 8HB
A CBS Company

A CIP catalogue record for this book is available from the British Library

ISBN   978-1-84738-848-3

Printed in China

1 3 5 7 9 10 8 6 4 2

CONTENTS

by Sarah Willson
illustrated by The Artifact Group

"Have a great trip!" said SpongeBob.
"I will water your plants
  while you are away!"
"Thanks," said Mermaidman.

"Feel free to borrow
the invisible bicycle–
if you can find it,"
added Barnacleboy.

"I will take care of everything,"
said SpongeBob.
"After all, you will only be gone
for two weeks.
What could go wrong?"

Meanwhile, in Plankton's lair . . .

Stinky Squ
Dirty Bubble
Slimy Pete
Terrible Tuna
Bad Blowfish
Ugly Urchin
Ghastly Grouper
Sinister Squid
Man Ray

"Aha! They are leaving town!"
said Plankton as he cackled.
"I will invite all the bad guys
to Bikini Bottom!"
He got on the phone and hit
every number on his speed dial.

The bad guys arrived quickly. "Welcome, fellow do-no-gooders!" said Plankton. "Mermaidman and Barnacleboy are out of town. Now we can take over the world!" All the bad guys nodded and laughed.

"And with those two out of the way,
I can finally get my hands on
that Krabby Patty formula!"
Plankton added to himself.

"I think I will go for a bike ride,"
said SpongeBob.
He looked around for
the invisible bicycle.

Three hours later, SpongeBob
found the bicycle.
He opened the garage door
and yelled, "Oh, no!"

Bikini Bottom was in big trouble!
"Help!" everyone cried.
"Where are Mermaidman
and Barnacleboy?"

BANK

Everyone was so scared,
they were leaving Bikini Bottom.
Even the police were running away!
SpongeBob knew that it was
up to him to save the day.
"This," he said, "is a job for . . ."

NOW
LEAVING
BiKiNi
BOTTOM

"Man Sponge!"

"Off I go to defend the weak, protect the helpless, and fight evil!" said Man Sponge. "To the invisible bicycle!"

"Wait. Where did I park it?" And one hour later, off he went.

"Stop, thief!" shouted Man Sponge.

But the thief did not stop.

"Well, that didn't work,"

Man Sponge said. "What do I do now?"

Just then the thief tripped over
the invisible bicycle.
The bag of money flew into
Man Sponge's hands.
"I did it!" he cried happily.
"Help!" someone else shouted.

Some bad guys had tied up
the ice-cream guy—and Patrick!
The bad guys were pushing all the
ice-cream tubs out of the truck!

Man Sponge crept up to the truck
and took the bad guys' rope.
Twirling it like a lasso, he caught
the two guys and tied them up.
Then he untied Patrick and the
ice-cream man.

Man Sponge saw someone ring
a doorbell, then run away.
He saw Man Ray pop bubble wrap
in the library!
He saw someone else paint on a sign.
"Freeze!" yelled Man Sponge.
But no one froze.

31

All these bad guys were heading
toward Man Sponge.
So he squirted bubble-blowing liquid
on the ground.

"Whoa!" yelled the bad guys.
They slipped and slid
on the bubble stuff—
right into Man Sponge's
huge jellyfishing net!

Suddenly Man Sponge heard "Help!"
It was Mr. Krabs.
"Somebody has stolen the secret
Krabby Patty formula!"
he yelled.

"It must be Plankton!" said Man Sponge.
He sprang into action.

"Stop, Plankton!" yelled Man Sponge.
But Plankton did not stop.
Man Sponge pulled something
out of his costume.
TWANG! His tightie-whities
knocked Plankton down.

THE KRUSTY KRAB

BUY

FREE

ENTER

Man Sponge trapped Plankton.
"That should hold you
    until the police return," he said.
"I will get you next time, Man Sponge,"
    said Plankton.

At last, all was well
in Bikini Bottom.
Everyone came back.
So did the police.
They put the bad guys behind bars.

"Thank you, Man Sponge!"
  everyone shouted.
"Aw, it was nothing,"
  said Man Sponge.

Two weeks later, Mermaidman and
Barnacleboy returned.
"How was everything?"
asked Mermaidman.
"Oh, just fine," said SpongeBob.
"Everything was under control!"

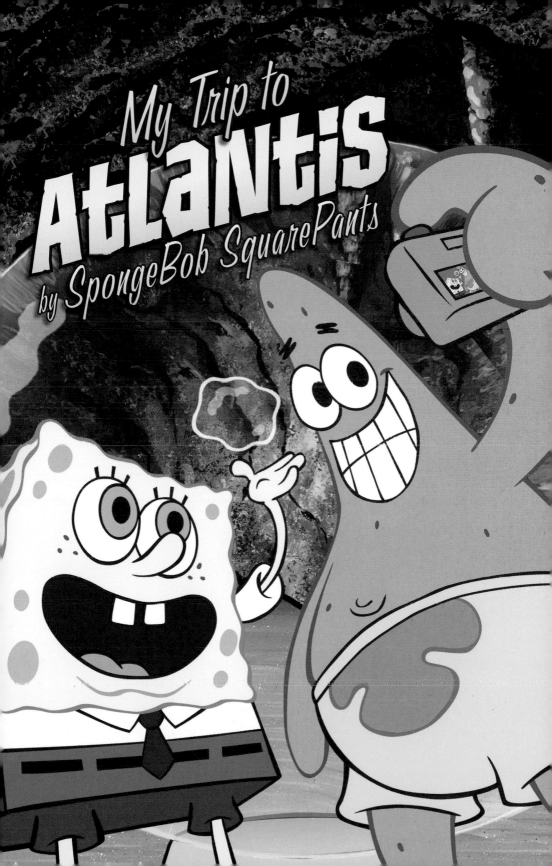

adapted by Sarah Willson
based on the teleplay
"Atlantis SquarePantis" by Dani Michaeli and Steven Banks
illustrated by The Artifact Group

It all began when I was blowing
bubbles with Patrick.
"Watch this, Patrick," I said.
I blew and blew. My bubble was huge!
But then it closed in around us and
began to float away—with us inside!

"Aaaah! What have I done?" I cried.

We floated for a long time.

We finally ended up in a cave.

That's when we heard a *pop*!

The bubble popped on something sharp!

"What is that? It looks like
an old coin," I said.
It looked ancient,
so we decided to take it to
the Bikini Bottom Museum.

We met Sandy and Squidward there.

"Where did you get that?"
Squidward asked.

"This old coin?" I said.

"That's the missing half of the
Atlantian amulet!" said Squidward.

We had no idea what he meant.
"Missing omelet?" asked Patrick.
"No, *amulet*! It is from the lost
city of Atlantis!" Squidward said.
Then he showed us a mural
of Atlantis on the wall.

"They say the streets of Atlantis
are paved in gold," said Squidward.
"What?" yelled Mr. Krabs.
He had just appeared out of nowhere!

Squidward told us that Atlantis was
known for its arts and sciences.
"They invented weapons, too.
But the people of Atlantis were
peaceful and never used them,"
he said.

"What's that bubble doing there?"
   I asked Squidward.
"That's the world's oldest bubble.
   The real bubble is in Atlantis."

Then Sandy had an idea.

"Connect the two halves!" she said.

"They might take us to Atlantis!"

So Squidward put them together.

There was a loud *boom*!

Then we saw bright beams of light.

All of a sudden a van appeared!
The amulet floated over to it
and clicked into place.
"All aboard!" said Sandy.
Zoom! We were flying!
We flew and flew until—*crash!*
We were finally there!

We saw a great big palace.

"Welcome to Atlantis!" a man said.

"I am King Lord Royal Highness."

"I am SpongeBob," I said.

"These are my friends."

"Would you care for a tour
    of our great city?" he asked.

    We all said yes, and off we went!

"For centuries we have been experts in art, science, weapons, and treasure collecting," said the king. Mr. Krabs jumped up and down. "I love treasures!" he said.

So the king took us to the
treasure room.
"Help yourself!" he told Mr. Krabs.
We left Mr. Krabs there.
Patrick and I just wanted to see
the world's oldest bubble.

Then Sandy asked to see
the Hall of Inventions.
The Atlantians had invented a lot!
They even had a machine that turned
everything into ice cream!
We left Sandy there to explore.
We kept looking for the bubble.

Squidward wanted to see the art.
We left him in the Hall of Arts.
Finally, I blurted out,
"Please, oh please, may we see
the ancient bubble?"
The king smiled. "Of course!"

"Behold our most beloved treasure,"
 the king said.
"This bubble is more than one million
 years old. Please be careful!"
The king left. We just stared.
"This is the most beautiful,
 wrinkled-up old bubble
 I have ever seen!" I said.

Patrick thought so too.
He decided to take a picture
of us with the bubble.

Click! Pop!

"Pat, did you hear something?"

Patrick and I looked at each other.

"Oh, no!" we both yelled.

"We destroyed the most ancient,
priceless treasure in Atlantis!
How will we tell the king?" I asked.

That evening at our dinner feast
we told the king about the bubble.
He just laughed.
"That's not the real bubble.
This is!" he said, showing it off.
But then Patrick took a picture of
the real bubble.
And this one popped too!

"We are so sorry!" I cried out.

The king's face just darkened.

"Guards!" he yelled.

"Do not let them get away!"

"RUN!" shouted Sandy.

We ran and ran.

The guards chased after us.

We ran straight into Plankton.
He was driving a huge tank.
"Cower before me!" he said
with an evil laugh. "Now I have
the most powerful weapon!
Prepare to taste my wrath!"

He pressed the button.
I was so afraid!
Splat!

"Plankton's wrath tastes like
    ice cream!" said Patrick.
"Mmm!" I said, shoveling it into my mouth.

"This thing blasts ICE CREAM?"
said Plankton angrily.
He climbed down and began
to kick the tank.
"OW!" he yelled.

We were happy that we were saved
from Plankton, but we knew the king
was still angry with us.

But then the king smiled.
"Look! A talking speck!" he said.
"It will make a great replacement
for our ruined national treasure."
"I will get you!" yelled Plankton
as the king picked him up.
"Yes, this is much better than our
dusty old bubble," he said.

We got back in the van.
We waved good-bye to the king.
He seemed so happy that we had come!

And that whole bubble thing worked out in the end too. Boy, Atlantis sure is a great place!

We waved good-bye to Plankton.
I hope he has as much fun in Atlantis
as we did!

NO FLASH
PHOTOS!

by Erica David
based on the teleplay "The Great Escape" by Paul Tibbitt,
Steven Banks, Luke Brookshier, and Nate Cash
illustrated by The Artifact Group

Woo-hoo! The big day was finally here.
Today was the Krusty Krab's
eleventy-seventh anniversary.
"I have so many great memories
of the Krusty Krab," I told Gary.

Love at First Bite

I remember my first Krabby Patty.
This was before I was even born!
Mom and Dad were looking for
a place to eat.

"How about this place?" Dad asked
as we stopped in front of the
Krusty Krab.
"What do you think, baby?"
Mom said. She did not
have to ask me twice!

"What would you like to eat?"
Mom asked. I looked out
through her belly button
at the menu board.
"Kwabbie Pabbie," I said.

GALLEY GRUB

KRABBY PATTY	$2.00
DOUBLE KRABBY PATTY	$3.00
W/ CHEESE	$3.50
KRABBY FRIES	$1.00
KRUSTY COMBO	$1.50
KRUSTY DELUXE	$4.00
SEAWEED SALAD	$2.00
KID'S KRABBY MEAL	$3.00
KRABBY DELIGHT	$3.50
BARNACLE KRISPS	$1.00
SOUP OF THE DAY	$1.50
CORAL BITS	$1.00

It was the most amazing thing
I had ever tasted!
It was love at first bite.

On my way to work I spotted
an old Krabby Patty wrapper.
It reminded me of the first time
I saw the Krusty Krab on TV.

THE
KRUSTY
KRAB

A Sack Full of Krabbies

I was sitting in front of the TV. Suddenly Krabby Patties popped onto the screen. They swirled around to a catchy song.

"Buy, buy, buy!" the song said.
Then Mr. Krabs appeared, dressed
like a doctor. "Go out and get a sack
full of Krabbies!" he said. "They are
good for your health."

Soon after, I got to go to the Krusty Krab again. Mom and Dad got us a whole tray of Krabby Patties.

I took one bite and my stomach
jumped for joy.
Mr. Krabs was right.
Krabby Patties **are** good for you!

At the Krusty Krab, Mr. Krabs
was very excited. He was
expecting a lot of people to show up
at the restaurant.

"Today's a big day," said Mr. Krabs.
"I want everyone to look out
for Plankton."
He had a feeling Plankton would try to
steal the secret Krabby Patty recipe
on this special day.
"Aye, aye, sir!" I replied.

"It's up to us to keep the Krabby Patty recipe safe," I said. "That reminds me of the day you told me the secret recipe, Mr. Krabs."

A Dream Come True

"One day Mr. Krabs called me into his office. He was going to share the Krabby Patty recipe. But first we had to go where no one would hear us."

"First Mr. Krabs led me outside.
We crossed a busy street.
We walked and walked.
Soon we reached the edge of
Bikini Bottom. Still we kept
walking. We hiked through
a jungle.

Then we marched
across a desert."

"Next we crossed an old rope bridge.
We walked until my feet hurt.
I was getting tired. But finally
we came back to the Krusty Krab."

"What?" Squidward said. "You and
   Mr. Krabs just walked in a big circle?
   That is crazy!"
"No, it was the best day of my life,"
   I said. "I learned the secret recipe.
   It was a fry cook's dream come true."

"Well, **my** dream come true was
the day before you moved to
Bikini Bottom," Squidward said.
"Ha, ha, ha," I replied. "I know you
are glad I moved here."

Love Your Neighbor

"I'll never forget the day I moved to Bikini Bottom," I said. "I looked at a lot of houses, but none of them felt like home. I was very sad."

FOR SALE

"Then the most incredible thing happened. A pineapple fell from the sky! It landed right next to Squidward's house."

"Then I met Patrick. You two were my new neighbors! And now I am glad to say that you are my friends."

The Wedding

"Hey, remember when I married Sandy?"
I asked my friends. I recalled that day
so clearly. Sandy walked toward me
wearing a beautiful white dress.
She looked so pretty!

"SpongeBob, do you take Sandy as your
   wife?" the wedding official asked.
"I do," I replied.
"Sandy, do you take SpongeBob as your
   husband?" he asked Sandy.
"Sure 'nuf!" she said.

"I now pronounce you sponge and squirrel," the wedding official said. I leaned in to give Sandy a big kiss— and bonked my nose on her helmet!

It turned out the wedding was just part of a play, but that was the best role I ever had. Well, besides the role of fry cook at the Krusty Krab!

Later Mr. Krabs opened the doors to a restaurant full of happy customers. "Ah, the Krusty Krab. It's the home of good food, good friends, and good times," I told Patrick.

"Happy eleventy-seventh anniversary, Krusty Krab!"

by Sarah Willson
illustrated by Harry Moore

"What's wrong, Pearl?"
asked SpongeBob.
"Tomorrow is Parents' Day at school,"
sobbed Pearl, "and my dad
wants to come!"

"But what is wrong with
Mr. Krabs coming?"
asked SpongeBob.

"He wears uncool clothes,"
said Pearl. "And he has bad manners.
My friends will laugh at me."

Just then Mr. Krabs called out,
"SpongeBob, get me some grub!"
"Yes, sir! Right away, sir!"
said SpongeBob.

SpongeBob went to the kitchen and
whipped up a Krabby Patty.

"Here you go, sir,"
said SpongeBob.

"Umph," said Mr. Krabs. He did not say
"thank you."

"You are right about Mr. Krabs,"
  Squidward said to Pearl.
"He does have bad manners.
  And his clothes are worn out.
  Maybe you need to go
  to a new school."

Pearl sobbed even more.
Suddenly there was a loud *r-rip!*
"Aw, barnacles! I split my pants again!"
said Mr. Krabs. "SpongeBob, get me
some more tape!"

"We will?" said Squidward.
"Oh, SpongeBob!" said Pearl.
"That would be just swell."

A short while later SpongeBob burst
into the office.
"Mr. Krabs! Guess what? The queen
is coming to the Krusty Krab!"
"Which queen?" asked Mr. Krabs.

"Oh, uh, just a queen," replied
SpongeBob. "But don't worry.
I will help you study this
manners book. You will know
just what to do."

They read the book.

Mr. Krabs learned to say "please."

He learned to say "thank you."

He learned how to greet someone politely.

"Good manners are hard work!"
grumbled Mr. Krabs.

The next day SpongeBob and
Squidward took Mr. Krabs
to the mall.
They helped him choose
a new outfit.

"Why do I need a new outfit?"
 asked Mr. Krabs.
"Because you are going to see
 the queen," SpongeBob replied.
"Oh, okay," said Mr. Krabs.

"You really stand out,
   Mr. Krabs," said Squidward.
"Why, thank you!" said Mr. Krabs.

"Hey, maybe you can wear this
to Parents' Day tomorrow too!"
SpongeBob said.

At lunchtime the queen arrived.
Mr. Krabs was so nervous
he did not notice that
the queen was really Squidward
all dressed up!

He greeted the "queen"
with a bow.
He held out her chair for her.
He said "please" and "thank you."
And he did not even charge her
for refills on water!

The next day SpongeBob picked up
Mr. Krabs.
"Do I look okay?" asked Mr. Krabs.
"You sure do!" said SpongeBob.

"Thank you, SpongeBob. I want Pearl
to be proud of me," said Mr. Krabs.
"I am sure she will be," said SpongeBob.

"Pearl, is that your dad
in that funny outfit?"
asked Pearl's friend Jen.
Pearl gasped. "No! I mean, it *can't* be!"
"Hello, Pearl!" said Mr. Krabs.
"Is this a friend of yours?"

He bowed low and then said,
"How do you do?"
Jen giggled.

Pearl watched her father greet
her friends. He bowed.

He said "please" and "thank you."
He even refilled her teacher's water glass!

Mr. Krabs tugged at SpongeBob's arm.
"Good manners are hard work,"
he whispered. "And these new clothes
feel tight. But I will do anything
for Pearl."

Pearl tugged at SpongeBob's
other arm.
"What did you do to my dad?"
she whispered. "He is acting weird!
Please change him back!"
SpongeBob was surprised,
but he said, "Okay, Pearl."

A while later Mr. Krabs came back,
wearing his old clothes.
"Oh, Daddy!" said Pearl.
"You look coral!"

Mr. Krabs beamed. "Lead me
to the grub!" he said.

"Thanks for trying, SpongeBob," said Pearl. "You are a true friend. But you really should think about getting a new tie."